Dedicated to everyone who dreams, young or old.
Reach for the stars!

On bright summer day,
little Jaden ran to his mom.
She looked at him with a smile,
Warm and calm.

"I've been thinking about my future!"
Little Jaden beamed.
"But I'm a little scared
that I won't be able to reach my dream."

Jaden's mom grinned,
Kind and bright
And reached down to give him a hug
That was snug and tight.

"*My little baby*," she sang
"*I believe you could do nearly anything.*"

"*So tell me, what do you want to do?*
Anything's possible - I believe in you."

Jaden tapped a finger to his chin
Wondering where he should even begin.

"*I could be a scientist!*"
He wondered out loud.
"*I could find cures or make robots,*
I think that would make me proud!"

"*Or I could work with animals!*"
Jaden said with a smile.
"*Play with jaguars, elephants, and giraffes,*
I'd love to do that for awhile!"

"*Or I could be an artist!*"
He said, thinking of his crayons.
"*I can draw lions and tigers,*
Or little bunnies and fawns!"

"*Or I could be a nurse like Dad!*"
Jaden remarked.
"*I can help so many people,*
And give them back their spark!"

"*Or maybe I could be a chef*,"
Jaden said, feeling his tummy grumble.
"*I could make tasty soups and pies,*
And even apple crumble!"

"*Or I could be an astronaut!*"
He said with a start.
"*I could touch the stars and see Mars -
The universe is a work of art!*"

With all these wonderful ideas in mind,
Jaden felt his heart sing.
"*Mommy, now that I think about it
I can do anything*!"

Now it's your turn!
What's your dream?
Draw it in the sky
For Jaden to smile at and beam!

Made in the USA
Columbia, SC
12 June 2024

37086792R00018